Baby Bear

goes to the

Beach

Lorette Broekstra

For my father

First published in Great Britain in hardback in 2000 by Brimax
First paperback edition published in Great Britain in 2002 by Brimax,
an imprint of Octopus Publishing Group Ltd
2-4 Heron Quays, London E14 4JP

Copyright © Lorette Broekstra 2002

Originally published in Australia in 2000 by Thomas C. Lothian Pty Ltd

ISBN 1 85854 291 x (hardback)
ISBN 1 85854 460 2 (paperback)

Printed in China

t was a lovely day and Baby Bear was going
to the beach with his mama and papa.
He had already packed his beach bag and
was waiting for Papa Bear to find his hat.

'This is a good spot,' said Baby Bear
when they got to the beach.

He sat down and unpacked his ball,
his bucket, his shovel and his sunscreen.

The water looked great, but Baby Bear
decided to build a sandcastle first.

He filled buckets with sand
and piled them higher and higher until
he had built a beautiful sandcastle.

'That looks great!' said Papa Bear.

'It's wonderful. All it needs is a special shell right there,'
said Mama Bear pointing to the top of the castle.
'You're right!' said Baby Bear and he set off to find one.

Baby Bear searched . . .

and searched.

'Phew! It's getting hot,' he said to himself.
'Time for a swim.'

Baby Bear ran and jumped into the sea.

He splashed about in the cool clear water,

on his back . . .

on his belly . . .

and THEN he dived right under.

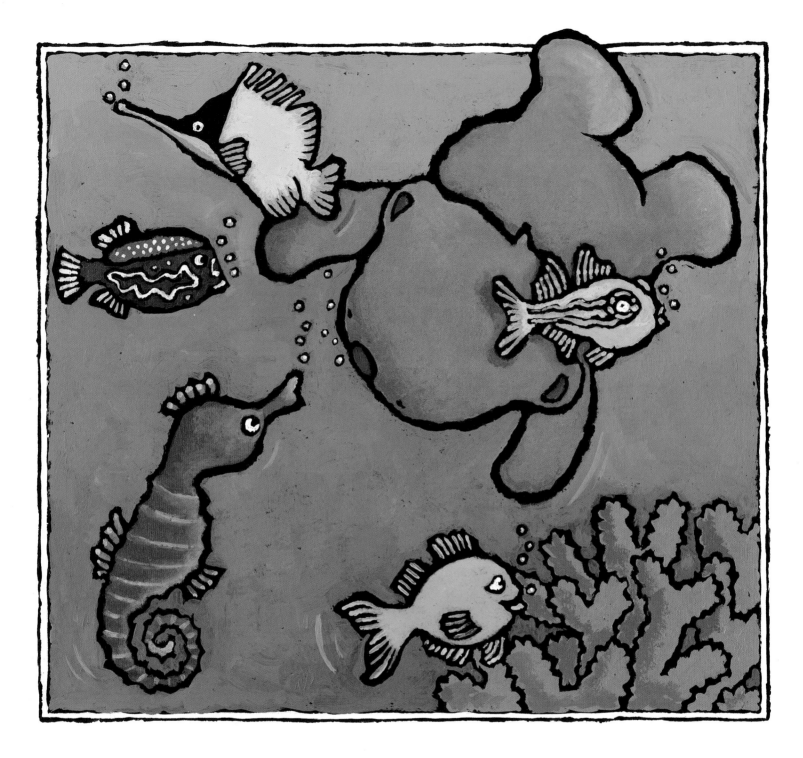

'Hello,' he said to a seahorse swimming by.
'Hello,' said the seahorse. 'Nice to meet you.'

'Ouch!' said Baby Bear when he felt
something nip him on the toe.
'Sorry,' said a crab, and he went on his way.

'You're in a hurry,' said Baby Bear to an octopus.
'Yes,' said the octopus, 'I can hardly keep up with myself.'

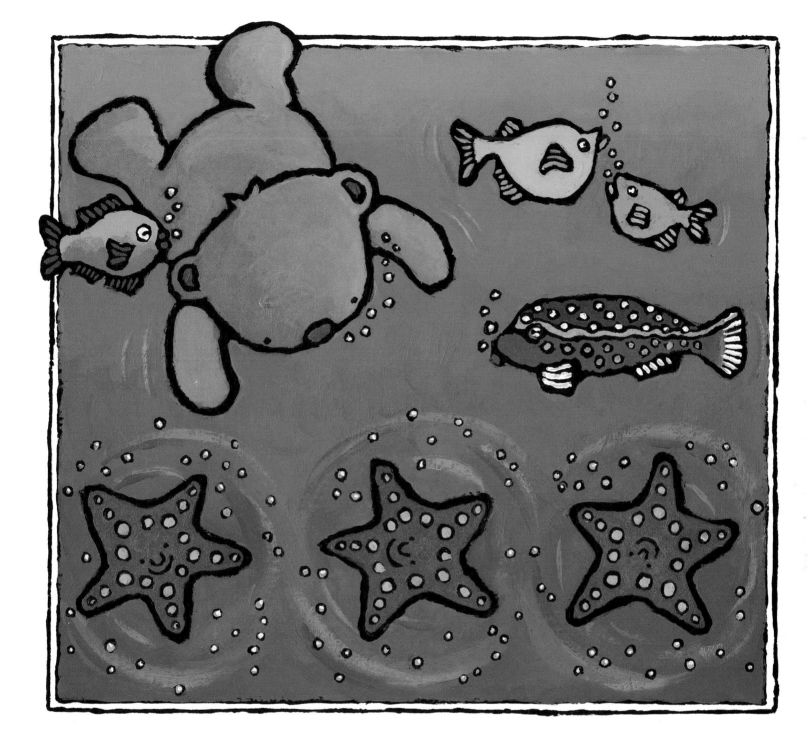

'That looks like fun,' said Baby Bear to a
spotted starfish doing cartwheels as he passed by.
'I'd like to try that.'

And he did a cartwheel, too.

He stopped when he heard a snap-snapping sound.
'Don't worry,' said a lobster. 'It's only me.'

Baby Bear clapped his hands when he saw
two jellyfish doing a lovely dance together.

'It's so beautiful down here,'
thought Baby Bear watching a school of fish
come swimming his way.

When they were gone Baby Bear looked down
and saw the most beautiful shell lying on the sea bed.
He'd found just what his sandcastle needed.

He picked up the shell

and quickly swam back

to find his mama and papa.

'Hi, Mama. Hi, Papa,' said Baby Bear.

'Hi,' said Mama Bear.

'What have you been doing?' asked Papa Bear.

'Oh, nothing much,' said Baby Bear,
'but I found a really nice shell for my sandcastle.'